Goggles for a Gloop

Enter into the world of a Gloop,
and follow his trail
as he learns a lesson in
trust and forgiveness.

copyright owner - Gloria Mezikofsky
Artful Dragon Press; printed in China
ISBN: 978-1-5136-5067-8

ARTFUL DRAGON
PRESS

Dedicated to nature lovers
with a heart for all little critters.

Gloria Mezikofsky, Writer

Merrill Mezikofsky, Illustrator

Lisa Mezikofsky, Designer

Russ Mezikofsky, Digital Artist

A Gloop is a very special critter who sits
on rocks and does nothing all day long;
well, almost nothing!

He does roll his fuzzy fur around different parts
of a rock that's bigger than three Gloops put together.
Can you imagine a rock that big?

Well, let me tell you a little secret.

Gloops are the size of a fuzzy cotton ball.

That's right!

A cotton ball!

That's really small!

Now, you must wonder what a Gloop

does all day long.

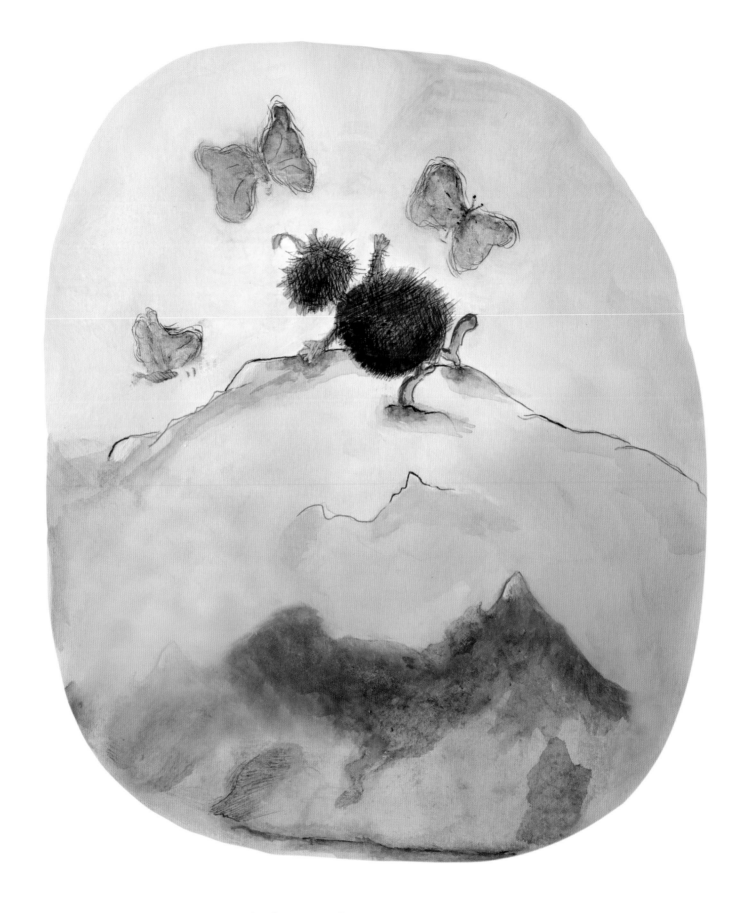

A Gloop has his eyes
On catching butterflies.

Falls on his fuzzy head;
Lands upside down instead.

He tries watching the sun go down.

Ends up with a mighty big frown.

Each and every day,

Mountains and trees get in the way.

They just swallow up the sun

When all is said and done.

Now, there's one Gloop who stands out from all the rest.

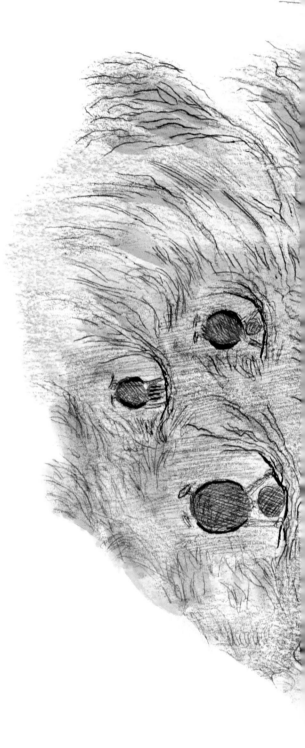

He's a very special Gloop.

His name is Gomer.

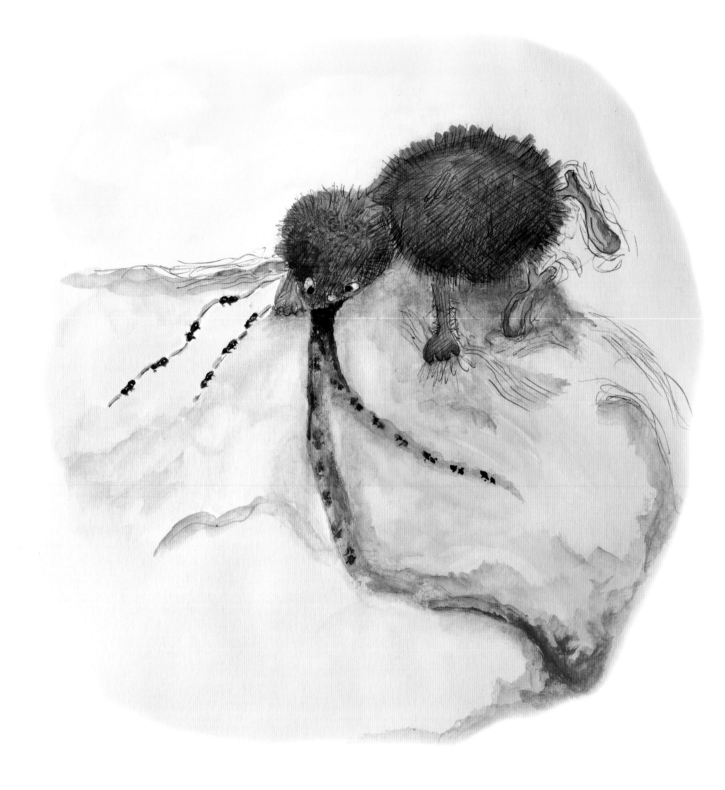

One day, Gomer decides to follow some creepy little ants up a hill and into a hole. He presses his face against the opening; looks down a long black tunnel. The hole is just too small for his fat fuzzy body.

So he decides to sit by the side of the hill watching the ants march in and out. "Hmm! Maybe that's it!" says Gomer. "There must be more to do down there, because there's nothing to do up here."

He begins digging a hole by the side of an anthill and doesn't see the little critters crawl all over his skinny legs. When he bends over to scratch his itchy body, some ants climb right on top of Gomer's fuzzy head.

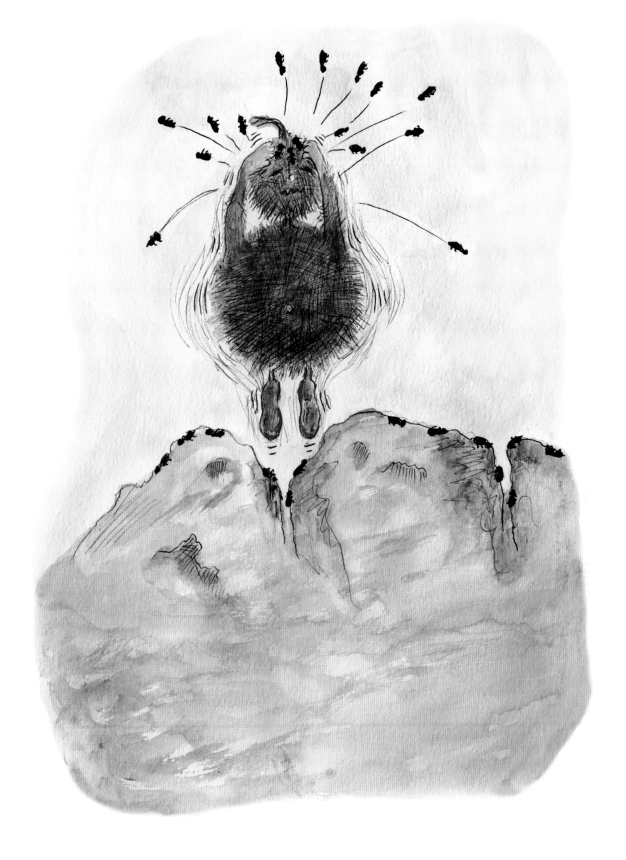

He jumps up and shakes himself off;
frantically pulling ants out of his hair.

Then he flings himself into a nearby puddle.

Why, he sure is the funniest looking Gloop you ever saw!

As soon as he rids himself of ants, he runs back looking for the anthill, but it's gone!

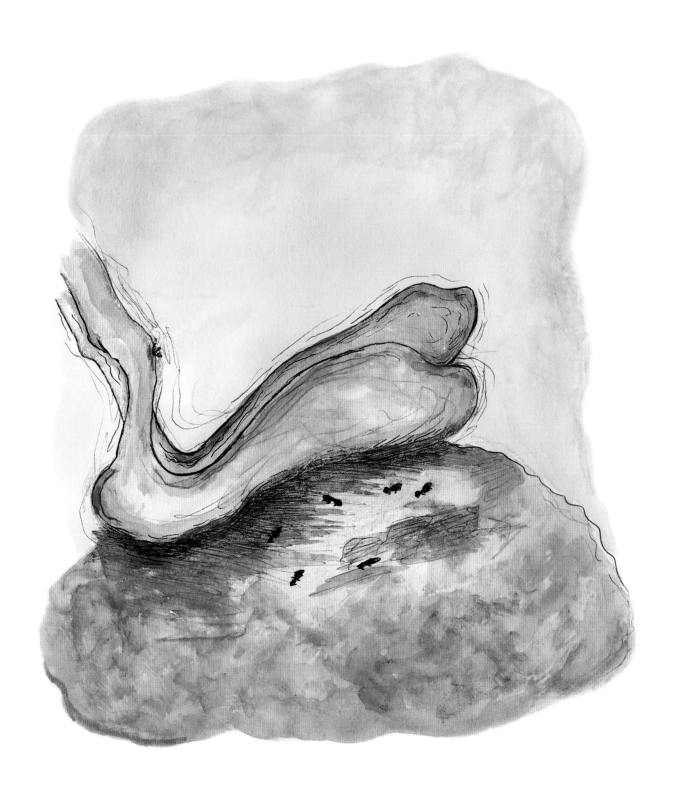

He forgets he crushed it to bits
with his clumsy webbed feet.

Gomer is so lonely with nothing to do.
So, he picks up some long, dry grass and tastes it.
"Ecch-h-h!-like straw!"

Gloops don't eat straw;
Too tough on the jaw!

Jump in it? No fun! "Hmmm! I know!
I'll light a fire to keep me warm at night."

He rolls the grass back and forth
until it's too hot to touch. "Ouch!"

Then he tosses it onto the ground.
He forgets that one little piece of
straw can light up a whole field.

The flames begin to slowly spread out.
Gomer gets scared and runs into a tree,
but an old owl shouts with a loud "Hoot!"

He falls back near a rock, but a bird is perched on it.
He shoos Gomer away. "Can't you see our homes are
going up in flames?!?" The fire can now be seen
everywhere in the surrounding fields.

Gomer runs fast; well, as fast as his fuzzy legs
will go, until he bumps into a stranger.
The stranger looks like two popsicle sticks
with an egg stuck on top of it.
Attached to the egg are two round pieces
of glass connected to a triangle.

The stranger scoops up Gomer. "Why, don't be afraid.
I won't hurt you. I love to catch frogs 'n fish and small
critters like you. I'm just going to put you in this little
jar so I can bring you home with me."

"Oh no you're not!" Gomer squirms
loose and drops to the ground.

He picks up his fuzzy little legs and starts to run away
only to get caught in one of the heaviest rainstorms ever!
Ooops! Even the rock that's bigger than three Gloops
put together is too slippery to sit on.

"What's happening?!? I can't see!!
Is water gushing down from a tree?"

"No!! It's the fireman's hose!!" hollers the little boy.
"Go away!" shouts Gomer. "The sun hides from me.
The ants crawl all over me, and now you want to lock me
up in a glass jar! I'm a fuzzy Gloop. Leave me alone!"

"Okay. I'll find another pet to play with.
Who needs a grumpy Gloop?"
says the little boy.

When he runs to
watch the firemen
hose down the blazing field,
he drops his goggles on
a big boulder.

"Hmmmmm! Egghead!" says Gomer as he crawls onto
the slippery rock, and what do you think he almost sat on?
The little boy's goggles! He picks them up, and slips them
over his tiny nose. "Wow! The flames look so bright!
The sky's so blue!"

Kerplunk! Gomer slides off the rock and cracks the goggles.

"Uh, Oh!" When he sees the little boy running back,
he hides behind the boulder. "My glasses!" shouts the boy.
Gomer meekly pokes his head up. "I broke them."
He snickers. "Now you can't see pretty things either!"
"That's not true. I have many pairs of goggles. If you come
home with me, you can see bright colors, too!"

Gomer sits down and thinks about it. "Hmm-mm-m!
No home! No food! No friends! Maybe you're right.
I guess I have nothing to lose.
I could try wearing a pair of goggles."

"I'll go with you just so long as you
don't put me in that ugly jar."
"I promise."
"And one more thing.....
the fire is out, but the birds, owls and ants
lost everything. It's so sad."

"Can you help me clean up these fields?"
"Sure thing!" nodded the boy.

As the birds fly overhead,
Gomer begins to clear away
the dead branches.
They swoop down to snatch up
the twigs making new nests;
bigger and better than ever!

The old owl glares at Gomer from afar as rubble is being cleared from a hollow spot near a sturdy limb.

The owl then soars overhead
flapping his mighty wings
as he prepares for a landing
to nestle down in his new home.

Now Gomer and the little boy watch the ants wobble over the debris. They work steadily to clear a path helping the little critters easily reach their underground city.

The ants form a single line along the new
path as they tunnel their way back home.

The birds swoop down with flapping wings.
The old owl "Hoots!" Ants quietly wiggle over
the Gloop's big clumsy webbed feet.

It's their way of saying "Thank you" as Gomer
makes his way over the gigantic rock to his new home.
He's relieved to know they all forgive him.

He's the only Gloop who has goggles big
enough for three Gloops put together.
But when you really think about it,
how many Gloops wear goggles?

Merrill and Gloria, husband and wife team, are pleased to bring you their second children's book, ***Goggles for a Gloop***.

As illustrator, Merrill captures the essence of the lead character and overall landscape.

Gloria enjoys bringing her characters alive with a theme that draws every child into the story.

Their first book, ***A Perfectly Snowy Day***, marked the beginning of their collaboration combining Merrill's unique artistic skills and Gloria's love for the art of storytelling.